Bald Eaglets

written by VICTORIA MILES
illustrated by LORNA KEARNEY

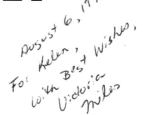

ORCA BOOK PUBLISHERS

In the branches of a Sitka spruce, a pair of bald eagles have built a platform of branches and twigs. This is their nest.

One eagle sits in the hollow of the nest, keeping the two large eggs tucked beneath her safe and warm. Her mate is nearby, ready to take his turn.

A faint chirping sound, *peep, peep!*, comes from one of the eggs. Against the inside of the shell wall, a small, sharp, horn-like tooth begins to tap.

The other egg is still.

This tapping continues for hours as the chick inside pecks tiny holes in the eggshell. Mother calls, *Kleek-kik-ik-ik-ik!*, and when Father arrives in the nest, she leaves to fly in the spring air.

Father nudges the eggs with his beak.
Pulling some soft greenery around
them, he settles down.

By midday, the tired eaglet has finally made a small crescent of holes in the shell. Struggling, she punches her beak through to the outside and pulls her tiny, wet body into the world.

The little bird collapses upon the soft carpet of green branch tips, seaweed and beach grass lining the nest. Her droopy eyes close and, snuggling into her father's feathers, she is soon warm, dry and fast asleep.

The next morning, Mother brings a fish to the nest and tramples upon it. With her beak, she tears off a small bite and holds it out gently. The eaglet cranes her weak neck upwards and grabs the piece of fish. *Peep! peep!*, she begs for more.

Two days go by. In the nest there is now a second empty eggshell and a little sister. The air is chilly, so Mother tucks the eaglets into her feathers while Father soars in the sky, searching for a fish in the water far below.

Father's sharp eyes spot a flash in the ocean. He swoops down, spreads his talons wide apart, breaks the water and grasps the fish with his feet. Beating his wings as hard as he can, he reaches a gust of wind that carries him back to the nest.

The two sisters grow quickly with each passing day. On fine days, the sisters play tug-of-war — each eaglet tries to wrestle a twig from the other's grasp. Big sister is a little bit stronger — she always wins.

After a few weeks, the eaglets have a thicker, woollier down to keep them warm.

On stormy days the tall tree sways back and forth in the wind. Mother stands over the eaglets, making a wide arch with her wings to protect them from the wind and rain. When the weather clears, Father and Mother collect sticks to repair the nest.

By midsummer, the eaglets will grow flight feathers to replace their fluffy down. Four or five winters will pass before they have white head and tail feathers and bright, clear, yellow eyes like their parents.

Indigenous to North America, bald eagles (*Haliaeetus leucocephalus*) are today estimated to number about 70,000 birds. As a result of declines due to pesticide poisoning, bounty programs and habitat loss, bald eagles have been listed as "threatened" or, more critically, as "endangered" over much of their original geographical range. Fortunately, strict protection and recovery efforts combined with relatively secure habitats in Alaska, British Columbia and Canada's boreal forest have granted the majority of bald eagles relative security today.

The author and illustrator are grateful for the contributions of conservationist Sherry Pettigrew, Registered Professional Biologists Michael Chutter and Richard Davies and wildlife biologist Ian Moul to this book.

For understanding
V.M.

Especially for Daniel
L.K.

Text copyright © 1995 Victoria Miles
Illustration copyright © 1995 Lorna Kearney

Publication assistance provided by The Canada Council.

Orca Book Publishers
PO Box 5626, Station B
Victoria, BC Canada
V8R 6S4

Orca Book Publishers
PO Box 468
Custer, WA   USA
98240-0468

10 9 8 7 6 5 4 3 2 1

Canadian Cataloguing in Publication Data
Miles, Victoria, 1966 —
    Bald eaglets

    ISBN 1-55143-028-2
    1. Bald eagle — Juvenile literature. I.
Kearney, Lorna, 1943– II. Title.
QL696.F32M54 1995   j598.9'16   C95–910216–

Design by Christine Toller
Printed and bound in Hong Kong